WHY THE POSSUM HAS A LARGE GRIN

WHY THE POSSUM HAS A LARGE GRIN

A Choctaw Tale Adapted by Johnette Downing
Illustrated by Christina Wald

PELICAN PUBLISHING COMPANY

Gretna 2012

For Walt Kelly, my early inspiration—C.W.

*The word "Pelican" and the depiction of a pelican are
trademarks of Pelican Publishing Company, Inc., and are
registered in the U.S. Patent and Trademark Office.*

Library of Congress Cataloging-in-Publication Data

Downing, Johnette.
  Why the possum has a large grin : a Choctaw tale /
adapted by Johnette Downing ; illustrated by Christina
Wald.
     p. cm.
  ISBN 978-1-4556-1639-8 (hc : alk. paper) —
ISBN 978-1-4556-1640-4 (e-book) 1. Choctaw Indians—Folklore.
2. Tricksters. I. Wald, Christina, ill. II. Title.
  E99.C8D68 2012
  398.20897'387—dc23
                          2011048313

Printed in Singapore
Published by Pelican Publishing Company, Inc.
1000 Burmaster Street, Gretna, Louisiana 70053

WHY THE POSSUM HAS A LARGE GRIN

Sometime past, there was one long, long, very long dry season north of Lake Pontchartrain in Louisiana. It was so dry that all of the bayous and lakes looked like the back of an alligator.

Now, that's dry.

Food was some kind of scarce, and the animals were having fits trying to find enough to eat.

It was there in the forest that the Deer, thin and hungry, came upon the Possum, who was smacking his wet lips together and rubbing his full belly.

Deer asked, "How are you so plump, Possum, when I can't find any food to eat?"

Possum looked at the tasty persimmon fruit hanging from the tree branches. "Ha, ha, ha!" said Possum with a sly smirk on his face. "Wouldn't you like to know?"

You see, ever since time began, the possum has enjoyed a reputation of being a little trickster.

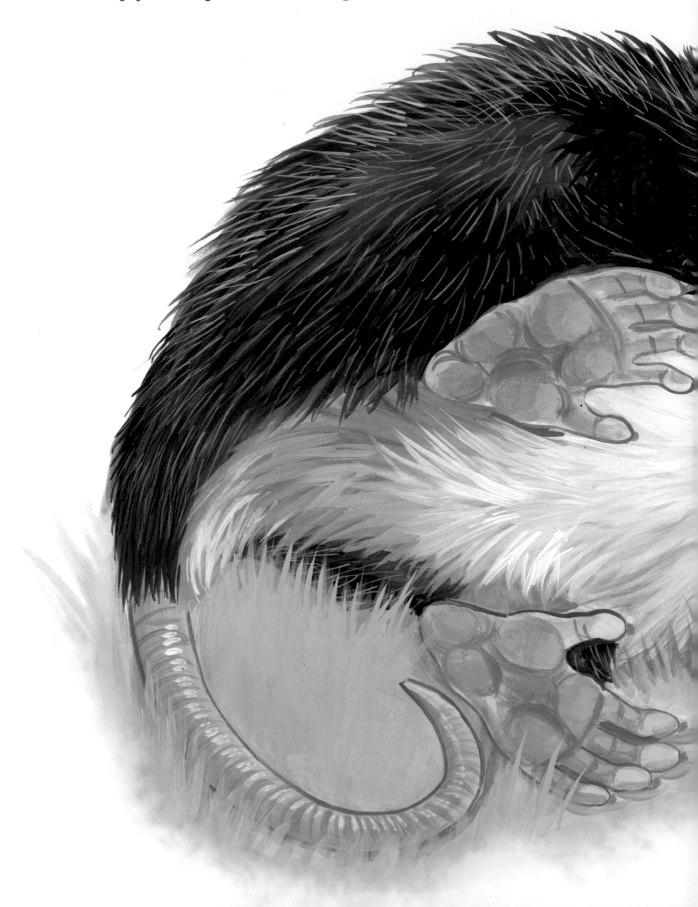

As cute as he is, he is not always one to be trusted. To make matters worse, Possum is some kind of lazy in the daytime and looks for any reason to get out of work so that he can take a nice cozy nap.

Possum could easily climb the tree and get some persimmons for the poor little Deer, but the mere idea of that long climb to help another soul just tired him out completely. Right then and there, Possum hatched a plan that would change the course of history forever.

Smelling the sweet fruit, Deer said, "Please help me, Possum. I am very hungry."

"Hmmmm," said Possum, followed by a hiss. "Okay, just *thissss* once, I'll help you. But you have to do everything I ssssay, just as I ssssay it."

Deer agreed.

Possum said, "It's really very simple. All you have to do is go to the top of that there hill and, running down as swiftly as those bony legs can carry you, hit this here persimmon tree so hard with your head that all of the ripe persimmons fall to the ground with ease."

"Once the persimmons are on the ground, you can eat and eat and eat until you can eat no more. But you have to do everything I ssssay, just as I ssssay it."

"That is easy indeed," answered Deer. "But won't it hurt if I hit my head on a tree?"

"It would hurt a small little possum like me if I hit my head on a tree, but you, so big and strong, you won't even feel it. But don't listen to me. I'll just eat this last persimmon and go to sleep while you go hungry."

"I'll do it!" said Deer.

"Suit yourself, but you have to do everything I ssssay, just as I sssssay it."

Deer agreed. Possum grinned, watched, and waited.

Deer went to the top of the hill just as Possum had instructed, turned, and ran quickly down, striking the tree with such force that two knots appeared on his head.

Sure enough, ripe persimmons fell from the tree and littered the ground.

When Possum saw the knots on Deer's head, he laughed and laughed. "Ha, ha, ha! Well my oh my, if that don't beat all! You did everything I ssssaid, just as I ssssaid it, and those bumps on your head are the funniest thing I have ever sssseen," declared Possum.

Possum rolled and rolled around in the grass, laughing at Deer.

He laughed so hard that he stretched his mouth in a grin forever.

Possum then picked up as many persimmons as his pouch could carry and left Deer to rub his aching head.

As the years passed, the two knots on Deer's head grew into horns.

And to this day, that is why the deer has antlers, and why the possum has a large grin.